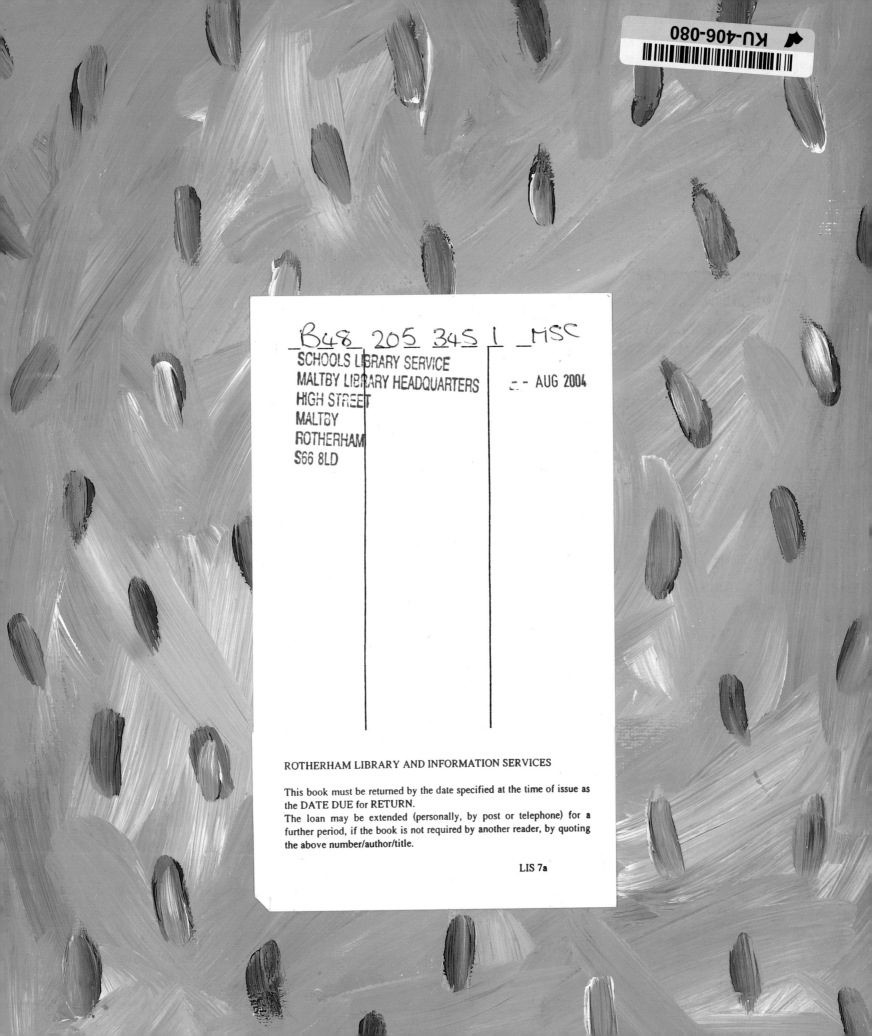

For Isaac and Honey

SIMON AND SCHUSTER

www.simonsays.co.uk

First published in Great Britain in 2004 by Simon & Schuster UK Ltd
Africa House, 64-78 Kingsway, London WC2B 6AH

Text and illustrations copyright © 2004 Jane Cabrera

The right of Jane Cabrera to be identified as the author
and illustrator of this work has been asserted by her in accordance
with the Copyright, Designsand Patents Act, 1988

Book designed by Genevieve Webster
The text for this book is set in Clarendon
The illustrations are rendered in acrylic paint

A CIP catalogue record for this book is available from
the British Library upon request

ISBN 0-689-86058-7

Printed in Italy

1 3 5 7 9 10 8 6 4 2

The
Pram Race

Jane Cabrera

Simon & Schuster
London New York Sydney

This is Banana Bob.

He likes to juggle bananas

. . . 1 2 3.

He likes to juggle for Radish and her little brothers
...1 2 3!

"Are you ready for the pram race?" asks Radish. "Yes," says Bob, "and I've made a banana cake for the winner!"

Banana Bob, Popcorn
and Pancake line up to
start the race.
"The first one back here is
the winner," shouts Radish.
"Ready, steady . . .

. . . GO!"
"Come on, you two!" shouts Bob as they
run under the banana trees.

"Hee hee, I'm winning!" laughs Bob
as they race through the sunflower field.

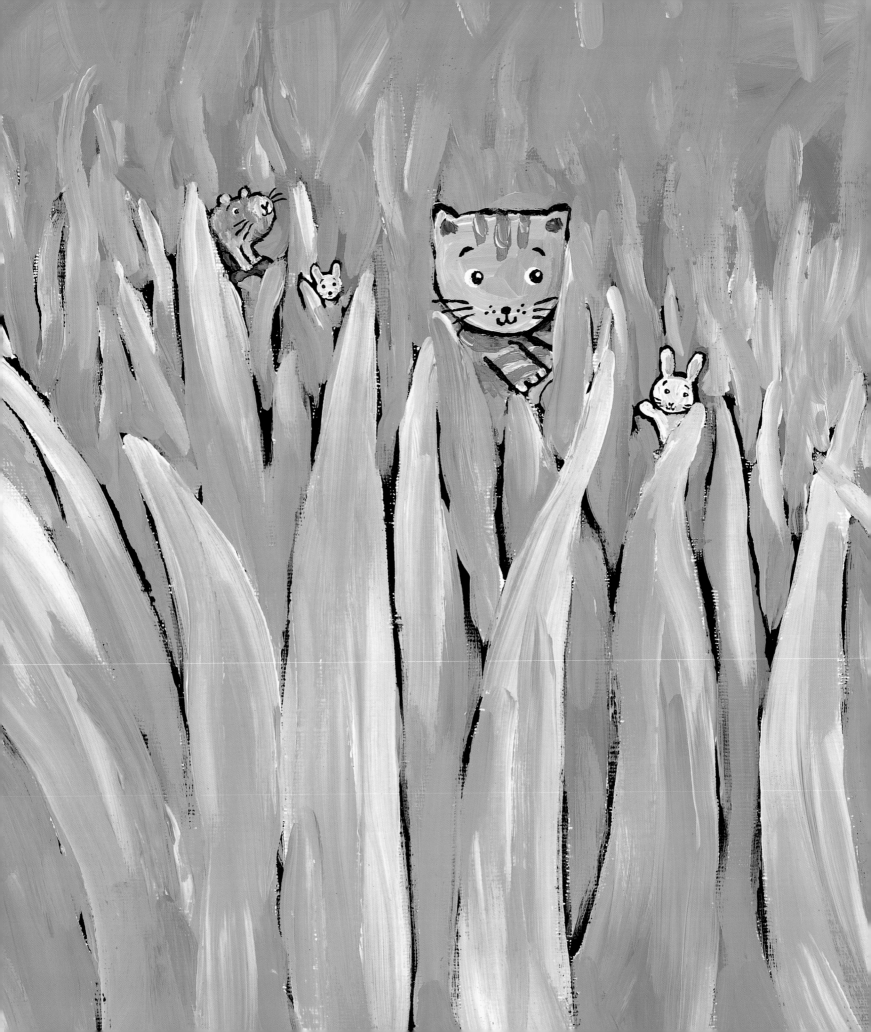

"I'm still in the lead!" pants Bob
as he dashes through the long grass.

"Keep up, slowcoaches!" jokes Bob as they zig-zag along the riverbank.

"You're winning," croaks
Korma as Bob races across
the rickety bridge.
"And you're nearly at the
finishing line!"

"Hooray!" laughs Radish,
waving her flag. "You're the winners."
"We've won, we've won!" shouts
the baby rabbit.
"Phew!" puffs Banana Bob.

Popcorn and Pancake aren't far behind . . .
"But where's Bob?" asks Popcorn.
"He should have the first slice of his
winner's cake."

"Here he is," giggle the baby rabbits.
"Wake up, Banana Bob!"

"We love pram races!"
laughs Bob.

"And we all love
your banana cake!"
says Popcorn.

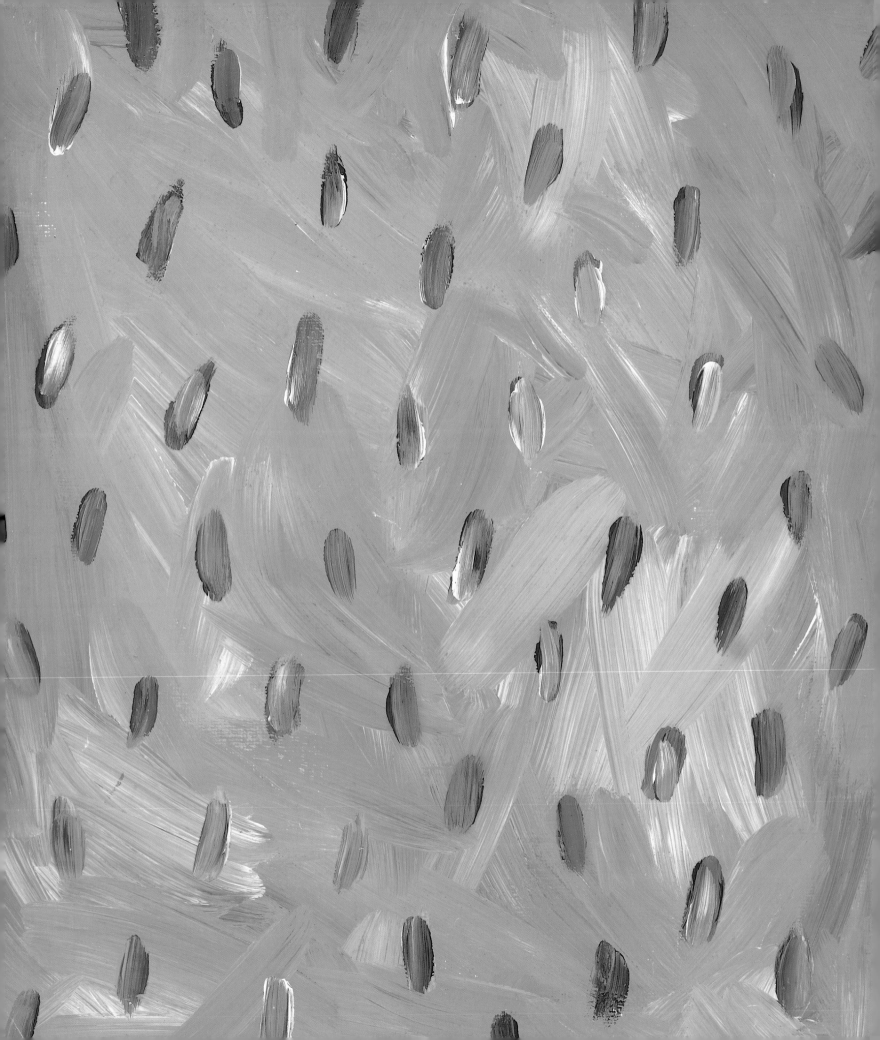